HURON COUNTY LIBRARY

The Merrythought

By the same author

THE CUCKOO CHILD
DODOS ARE FOREVER
FIND THE WHITE HORSE
THE GHOST AT CODLIN CASTLE
LADY DAISY
PADDY'S POT OF GOLD
PRETTY POLLY
THE WATER HORSE

DICK KING-SMITH

The Merrythought

—

Illustrated by Mike Reid

VIKING

VIKING

Published by the Penguin Group
Penguin Books Ltd, 27 Wrights Lane, London w8 5tz, England
Penguin Books USA Inc., 375 Hudson Street, New York, New York 10014, USA
Penguin Books Australia Ltd, Ringwood, Victoria, Australia
Penguin Books Canada Ltd, 10 Alcorn Avenue, Toronto, Ontario, Canada m4v 3b2
Penguin Books (NZ) Ltd, 182–190 Wairau Road, Auckland 10, New Zealand

Penguin Books Ltd, Registered Offices: Harmondsworth, Middlesex, England

First published 1993
1 3 5 7 9 10 8 6 4 2
First edition

Typeset by Datix International Limited, Bungay, Suffolk
Filmset in 13/16 pt Monophoto Baskerville
Printed in England by Clays Ltd, St Ives plc

A CIP catalogue record for this book is available from the British Library

isbn 0–670–83688–5

Contents

Chapter 1	Nick's First Wish	7
Chapter 2	Win Some, Lose Some	17
Chapter 3	Testing, Testing	24
Chapter 4	In the Dustbin	31
Chapter 5	'Could Do Better'	38
Chapter 6	Dangerous Hill	45
Chapter 7	'Yours for 50p'	53
Chapter 8	One Bad Wish	62
Chapter 9	A List of Presents	69
Chapter 10	Start the Clock	79
Chapter 11	Birthday Surprise	85
Chapter 12	Bon Voyage	95
Chapter 13	The More, the Merrier	105
Chapter 14	Happy Christmas	109

CHAPTER 1
Nick's First Wish

'For what we are about to receive,' said the Vicar, 'may the Lord make us truly thankful.'

He picked up the carving knife and began to sharpen it upon the steel. 'Which I certainly shall be,' he went on, 'after that sermon.'

His wife laughed. It was one of the Vicar's regular jokes that preaching his sermon on the theme of the Feeding of the Five Thousand made him feel very hungry.

Nick laughed because, being the oldest at nine, he had heard the sermon and the joke several times before.

As for the two sets of twins, the six-year-old pair, Cassandra and Josh, didn't laugh because they had paid no attention to what their father had said from the pulpit since they had been busy reading *Thomas the Tank Engine* and *Toby the Tram Engine*.

The four-year-old boys, Denny and Tim, who had been taken out of church before the sermon anyway, remained silent, their eyes fixed unwaveringly upon the roast chicken. It was a very large chicken. It had to be, for as the Vicar's wife often said, 'Feeding this lot's bad enough, never mind the Five Thousand.' She often gave them chicken for Sunday lunch, partly because everyone liked it, partly because of the ceremony of the wishbone. Pulling the wishbone was a family tradition, and the children took turns at it, in order of age. At first, of course, Nick had no competition, but as each set of twins grew old enough, they joined in.

Cassandra and Josh were known jointly as the Old Twins, Denny and Tim as the New Twins. Confusingly for visitors to the Vicarage, OT and NT did not refer to the Testaments.

When it was the OTs' turn for the wishbone, they pulled against one another, and likewise with the NTs. Nick would pull against one of his parents.

The Vicar was an expert carver, and when he had dismembered the bird, he neatly removed the V-shaped bone from the top of the breast, and held it up.

'Now then,' he said, 'whose turn is it for the merrythought?'

'Ours!' said the OTs and the NTs with one voice, but Nick said, 'No, it's not, Dad, it's mine. The NTs got it last time we had chicken.'

'Yes, they did,' his mother said.

'All right,' said the Vicar, and holding the bone by one end, he offered the other to Nick.

'Come on then,' he said.

They pulled, and the wishbone broke with a little crack. Nick had the longer part.

All the twins cheered.

'Make your wish,' their mother said.

'Why is it called a merrythought, Mum?' Cassandra asked.

'Well, the story is that, as well as having a wish granted, the person who gets the longer bit will be the first to get married. Which is a merry thought, I suppose.'

'That can't be right this time,' said Josh. 'Dad's married already.'

'What did you wish, Nick?' said the NTs together.

'You mustn't tell them,' said his mother. 'It spoils the wish if you do.'

'I'm not going to,' said Nick.

In fact, he hadn't wished anything. Whenever I've won it before and wished, it's never worked, he thought. I've never got the things I wished for – new bike, a skateboard, a computer. It's just a silly old superstition like so many others. Having good luck if a black cat crosses your path (only it must be going

9

from right to left), or if you meet a chimney-sweep and then keep your fingers crossed until you see a dog's tail. Load of rubbish.

He put the piece of bone on the side of his plate and went on eating.

After Sunday lunch the routine at the Vicarage was always the same. It was called 'Dad's Quiet Time', when the Vicar went to his study to 'prepare himself for Evensong', which meant a nice long nap in a comfy armchair. Meanwhile, the NTs went to their beds for a rest, and the OTs were made to be still and quiet with books or drawing-paper. Nick helped his mother with the washing-up.

A part of his duties was to scrape any leavings (not that there were many) from the plates into a bowl, for the family dog, a greedy and unfussy little terrier named Piglet, who ate everything put in front of him.

'Look out for bones, Nick,' his mother said. 'Chicken bones splinter like anything and we don't want to condemn Piglet to an early death.'

Thus it was that Nick, sifting through the leftovers, came upon the two bits of the merrythought.

Quite why he picked out both parts and slipped them into his trouser pocket without his mother seeing, he did not know. But this is what he did, before putting the other bones in the dustbin.

The washing-up done, Nick went upstairs to his bedroom and took down his dictionary from the bookshelf.

Wishing-Bone, wishbone.   [*he read*]

The V-shaped bone formed by the fused clavicles in a bird's breast, the merrythought, pulled apart in playful divination.

He looked up the meanings of 'fused', 'clavicles' and 'divination'. Then he took the two bits of bone out of his pocket and looked at them, and an idea struck him.

Suppose everyone's always been wrong about this, he thought. In breaking the wishbone, I mean. How can it matter who gets the long bit – for example, today I could have made a wish that didn't come true and Dad could have made one with the short bit and had it granted. Suppose the magic (because it is magic, after all, isn't it, to have a wish come true?) only works for the whole wishbone, the whole merrythought? Bet no one's ever thought of trying that!

A quarter of an hour later the job was complete. It was just the kind of thing that Nick, a keen model-maker, was good at doing. He had washed

both pieces of bone carefully to get off any grease or shreds of meat, dried them thoroughly and then, very precisely, joined them back together with super-glue. The break had been clean and the union was a perfect one. The merrythought looked as good as new.

Shall I have a go with it, Nick thought? After all, I didn't wish a wish at lunchtime, when I got the longer bit. I'm sort of owed one.

But then he heard the OTs coming upstairs, calling his name. Dad's Quiet Time was over, and they would, he knew, want him to come and kick a football about on the lawn. Josh fancied himself as a goalkeeper, and Cassandra packed a mean left foot.

Nick found a little cardboard box amongst his modelling kit, popped the merrythought in it, and put the box away in a drawer.

At teatime the conversation turned once again to wishes.

'I've an idea for my sermon for next Sunday,' said the Vicar to his wife.

'Oh good,' she said.

Oh good, she thought, he does tend to trot out the same old themes. It'll make a change to hear something quite fresh.

'What is it?' she asked.

'Well, it came from thinking about pulling that wishbone at lunch. I don't know what Nick wished, and I certainly shan't ask him, but I bet one thing.'

'What, Dad?' said Nick.

'I bet it was selfish.'

'How d'you mean?' his wife said.

'What I mean,' said the Vicar, 'is that we very often say "I wish something or other", and almost always it's something that is purely and simply for ourselves. For example, Nick might have said to himself "I wish I had a new bike".'

'I wish we had,' said the OTs.

'You're all right,' said Josh to his sister. 'You'll get a new girl's one – I'll just get Nick's old one.'

'We haven't got bikes,' said the NTs.

'You're too small,' said the OTs.

'You see?' said the Vicar.

'Wishes are a bit like prayers in a way, I suppose,' he went on. 'We all tend to pray selfishly – "keep me safe, help me, comfort me, watch over me".'

Absently he crumbled a slice of cake in his fingers and a piece of it fell under the table, where Piglet flung himself on it like a hungry shark.

'Well we do pray for other people too,' his wife said. 'For the sick and the bereaved and all sorts of people less fortunate than we are. Surely prayers are not all selfish?'

'No, but nor should wishes be,' said her husband. 'That's exactly my point. How nice it would be if, next time one of us pulls the wishbone and gets the longer part, he or she makes a wish, not for themselves, but for someone else.'

'Well, suppose you'd won today, Dad,' Nick said. 'Who would you have made a wish for?'

14

'Let's see,' said the Vicar. He crumbled some more cake, to Piglet's joy. 'Well if I'm to follow my own preaching,' he said, 'I suppose I'd have made a wish for Mr Pargeter's old mother.'

'Mr Pargeter at the village shop?' his wife said.

'Yes. His old mother – she must be nearly ninety – caught a chill and it's turned to pneumonia. There's no hope, they say. In fact I'm half expecting to be called to the Cottage Hospital some time this evening. So I'd have wished for her to pass peacefully away.'

When his father had gone off to conduct Evensong, Nick went up to his room. He shut the door, and opened first the drawer and then the box, and took out the merrythought.

He held it by the tips of the arms of the V, between finger and thumb, as a dowser might hold his divining-rod when searching for water. He stared at it. He spoke.

'I wish,' said Nick, 'that old Mrs Pargeter would get better.'

Though he could have sworn that he had not moved it, he felt the merrythought give a little twitch.

Later that evening, when all five children were in bed and asleep, the telephone rang.

'Who was that?' asked the Vicar's wife when he had answered it. 'You sounded very surprised.'

'I am!' said the Vicar. 'That was Pargeter. No need for me to go to the Cottage Hospital. His old mother is sitting up in bed, drinking a large glass of stout.'

CHAPTER 2
Win Some, Lose Some

Nick heard about Mrs Pargeter at breakfast next morning.

He had not known quite how to bring the subject up, so he decided on a direct approach.

'Dad,' he said, 'did old Mrs Pargeter pass peacefully away?'

'Not a bit of it,' said the Vicar. 'She's miles better.'

'Oh,' said Nick.

'I'm glad she didn't die,' he said.

'She will sooner or later,' said Josh.

'Everybody does,' said Cassandra.

The NTs looked worried at this OT prophecy, and their mother hastened to put in some cheering words.

'But not until they're really old,' she said.

'Mrs Pargeter *is* old,' said Josh.

'*Very* old,' said Cassandra.

'What a gloomy pair you are,' said the Vicar. 'Why, she'll probably live to be a hundred!'

She might too, thought Nick. If the merrythought worked once, it might work again if she needs it.

In his room, he took the wishbone out of its box and sat on his bed, holding it by its ends.

'Just think,' he said to Piglet who had followed him upstairs. 'This thing saved old Mrs Pargeter's life!'

Despite all Nick's cleaning of it, the merrythought apparently still smelt attractive to the ever-hungry Piglet, and now he sat upright on his bottom – a posture that was easy for such a fat, short-legged beast – and begged for it.

'You're not having this!' Nick said.

Piglet whined, licking his lips, his eyes fixed on the wishbone as eagerly as if it was a T-bone steak.

'I wish you weren't so greedy, Piglet,' said Nick.

It was not until he felt the merrythought twitch that he realized what he had said.

It was with a feeling of awe that Nick watched what happened when Piglet was fed. His usual supper of meat and biscuit was set before him in his usual dish, a brown earthenware bowl which, as it happened, was inscribed RABBIT.

Normally Piglet dashed at this dish and sank his

head into it, and with open jaws and convulsive jerks of his shoulders, threw the food into himself in less than half a minute.

But now, when Nick's mother put the food down, Piglet approached quite slowly and sniffed at the dish before beginning to eat, delicately, like a cat. He ate perhaps half his supper and turned away.

'Whatever's the matter with him?' Nick's mother said. 'I've never known him leave his food before, not in all his life. In fact, I've never known him leave a crumb. He must be ill.'

He may be, thought Nick. But he may just not be so greedy as he was!

Of course it could be pure chance, he said to himself. Old Mrs Pargeter might have got better because they gave her antibiotics and stuff. Piglet might just be off his food, for once.

But as the days passed, it became plain that Piglet was a changed dog. No longer did he wait, dribbling, underneath the table at every mealtime, nor haunt the kitchen between meals; and his own rations, because he never seemed able to finish them, were now halved. He began to look quite trim.

'He doesn't seem ill,' the Vicar said. 'His nose is cold and his eyes are bright, and in fact he's much more active than he was.'

'Because he's nothing like as fat,' his wife said. 'I suppose I was over feeding him. Isn't it odd – it's as though he'd put himself on a diet.'

*

Now as the week went by, and Mrs Pargeter was discharged from the Cottage Hospital, and Piglet continued to eat a great deal less than usual, Nick began to believe that he had something very, very special in that box in his room, nothing less in fact than a magic object capable of granting wishes.

But did it depend what sort of wishes?

He remembered what his father had said, about selfish and unselfish ones. So far he had done nothing selfish – the merrythought had been used only for the good of old Mrs Pargeter and Piglet. Maybe it was time he wished for something for himself. Nothing too big, Nick thought, just a smallish thing.

He was lying in bed on the Friday morning, thinking all this, when he heard his mother's voice.

'Nick!' she called. 'Hurry up! Everyone else has nearly finished breakfast. You're going to be late for school.'

School, thought Nick . . . Friday . . . football, and as he hurriedly dressed, the perfect modest little wish came into his head.

There was to be a football match later that afternoon against a school from a neighbouring village. Nick was an average sort of footballer, a bit young for the First XI and not really good enough, but that didn't matter, did it! The merrythought would get him into the side today, somehow!

He took it out of its box, held it up in the proper manner, and was about to say that he wished he could play for the school today, when it occurred to him that he could improve on that.

'I wish,' said Nick, 'that I could play for the First
XI today and score a goal.'

Twitch, went the merrythought.

As soon as he got to school, Nick hurried to the
notice-board. The team was posted up. His name
was not on it.

But even as he stood, doubly disappointed, an
arm came over his head and a hand with a pen in it
crossed out two names.

'This dratted flu epidemic,' said the voice of the
games teacher. 'Now I've got to find two substi-
tutes.'

He looked down and caught Nick's imploring eye.

'OK, Nick,' he said. 'You can be one of them.
You'll be a defender, right? It's your big chance!'

After the match, the games teacher drove round
dropping off the members of the team at their various
homes.

At the Vicarage the OTs, who knew of course of
their brother's selection, came rushing out to greet
him.

'Did you win?' cried Cassandra.

Nick shook his head.

'What was the score?' asked Josh.

'1–0 to them,' said Nick.

The NTs arrived on the scene. They looked with
interest at Nick in his football gear.

'His knees are dirty,' said Denny to Tim.

'I 'spect he fell down,' said Tim to Denny.

'Did you win?' they said.

'Oh, shut up,' said Nick.

'Nick played for the First XI today, Dad,' said the OTs to their father later.

'Oh, jolly good,' said the Vicar. 'Did you score a goal, Nick?'

'Yes,' said Nick glumly.

'But you said they did!' cried Josh.

'You said it was 1–0 to them,' said Cassandra.

'It was,' said Nick. 'The ball came off me. It was an own goal.'

CHAPTER 3
Testing, Testing

Nick could sometimes behave in as silly or thought-less a way as any other nine-year-old boy, but in general he was quite a responsible person. Maybe it had to do with his being the eldest of the tribe, for even at the tender age of five, when the OTs were two and the NTs had only just arrived, he had told his grandparents, 'I'm the oldest, so Mummy and Daddy say I've got to act sensibly.'

Acting sensibly about the magic merrythought was now much on his mind. The merrythought could grant whatever he wished. Of that he was pretty sure. But was that because *he* wished it, or was it a talisman that anyone could use? Suppose Cassandra wished on it, or Josh? Would it work for them? And would they be capable of making sensible wishes? As for Denny and Tim, Nick shuddered to think what might happen. Both were mad on animals, especially – because of a book they'd been given – large African animals, and they would certainly jump at the idea of being able to order them by magic. A nightmare picture came into Nick's mind of rhinoceroses grazing the lawn, elephants and giraffes browsing on the trees, and hippos wallowing in the stream that ran at the bottom of the Vicarage garden.

Mind you, if either pair of twins got hold of the merrythought, it might not occur to them to wish or, if they did, they might not hold it correctly. And anyway it wasn't very likely that Cassandra or Josh would come nosing about in his top drawer, and Denny and Tim couldn't reach it. But it's better to be safe than sorry, thought Nick. I'd better find a hiding-place for it.

And then suddenly the perfect solution came to him. No need to hide the merrythought. All he had to do was enlist its help.

He took it out, held it up, and made his fourth demand of it.

'I wish,' he said, 'that neither my sister Cassandra nor my brothers Josh, Denny and Tim shall ever take you out of this drawer,' and the merrythought acknowledged this in the usual way.

The next night Nick was reading in bed. It was quite late and he was supposed to have turned out

his light and gone to sleep, but in fact he was reading under the bedclothes by the light of a little pencil-torch. The battery was on the blink, and the beam yellowed and dimmed and finally went out.

Suppose the power in my wishbone is like the power of that battery, Nick thought, just before he drifted into sleep. Suppose it only works for a certain time and then becomes useless? It's Sunday tomorrow. I'll get a spare.

But that Sunday's lunch was roast beef, and it was a further week before another chicken appeared on the Vicarage dining-table. It was of course the OTs turn to pull the wishbone.

Nick found himself hoping that Josh would win,

not because he was a boy, but because Cassandra was rather a bad loser, who would begin by sulking and end by pestering her brother to tell her what he had wished in hope of spoiling it. But today it was Cassandra who got the longer part.

It won't work, Cass, Nick said to himself as he watched her making her wish, eyes screwed up, and frowning furiously with the effort, you have to have the whole merrythought.

Which is what, later, he had. Once again he rescued the two parts from the leftovers, once again prepared and joined them. Now he had his spare.

'I'd better test you to make sure you work,' he said to it. 'Let's see, what shall it be?'

Nick stared out of his bedroom window, thinking. It was a pouring wet day, the kind that looks as though the rain will never stop, and the Vicar had thought fit to preach his sermon based upon the story of Noah's Ark to his damp congregation.

Nick looked out at the dark clouds and the unceasing downpour, wondering what to do with the rest of the Sunday afternoon. Dad's Quiet Time will be over soon, he thought, and what I'd like to do is to go down to the stream and fish for tiddlers. But I'll get absolutely soaked.

Then he thought, oh no, I won't! I'll soon fix that.

He picked up the spare merrythought by its ends.

'I wish the rain would stop,' said Nick. He waited for the spare wishbone to twitch, but it remained motionless. Instead, there was a sudden dazzle of lightning and a tremendous clap of thunder that woke the Vicar from his preparation for Evensong and set the NTs howling for their mother. The rain, if anything, doubled in volume.

The OTs came rushing into Nick's room.

'Did you see the lightning?' they said.

'Yes.'

'Lightning can kill you,' said Cassandra.

'You frizzle up,' said Josh. 'Like a burnt sausage.'

'What have you got in your hand?' said Cassandra.

'The wishbone you pulled at lunch.'

'You've mended it,' said Josh.

'Yes.'

'Why?' they said.

'Oh, just for fun. Here, you can have it. I don't want it. It's no use to me.'

So the OTs pulled it again and it broke at the same place, but this time Josh got the longer part, and then they quarrelled about that until Nick took both bits away from them, and put them in his pocket.

'If you two stop squabbling,' he said, 'you can come down to the stream with me and we'll catch some minnows.'

'But it's raining buckets!' they said.

'It'll stop in a couple of minutes,' said Nick. 'Go and get your wellies on. I'll be down soon.'

When they had gone, he took the original merry-

thought from its box. Outside, the rain was hammering down just as hard.

'Maybe this is the kind of thing that no wishbone can grant,' he said, 'or maybe you can do it because you are the one and only magic merrythought in the world,' and then once again he said, 'I wish the rain would stop.'

Even as the bone twitched, the drumming noise of the downpour ceased abruptly, and rushing to the window, Nick saw the last few drops fall from a sky that suddenly lightened with a gleam of sunshine.

The three children stood on the bank of the stream, Nick with his home-made fishing-rod, the OTs with nets. Nick had some bread for bait. He put his hand in his pocket to take it out and touched the two bits of the useless wishbone. He threw them into the depths of the sun-dappled water.

'You *said* the rain would stop, didn't you, Nick?' said Cassandra.

' "In a couple of minutes," you said,' Josh added.

'And it did!'

'It was just like magic!'

Nick grinned as he fitted a bread-pill on to the bent pin on the end of his line.

'It was, wasn't it?' he said.

CHAPTER 4

In the Dustbin

Fish as they might, they caught nothing that afternoon. Little did the OTs know that all Nick had to do was to pop back up to his bedroom for a few moments and then their jam jars would soon have been full of minnows and sticklebacks and anything else he cared to name.

Why, I could have wished for a proper fish, a big one, a salmon even, thought Nick afterwards. He'd eaten some once, and decided it was delicious. Though I don't quite know how I'd catch a salmon with my tackle. The merrythought would fix it somehow, I suppose. It's probably best to ask for a little one.

Next day he did just that.

'I wish for a little salmon,' he said to the merry-thought, and went down to the stream with his rod and a fast-beating heart.

For half an hour he stood in the stream, as far out as he could without the water coming over his wellies, for he thought that even a little salmon would need that much depth. The stream was clear, and now and then he could see tiddlers nibbling at his bait, but none took it. Of a salmon there was no sign.

At his mother's call to tea, he walked up the lawn disappointed, but with his faith undimmed. Perhaps the merrythought wouldn't always grant the wish immediately. Perhaps it would happen later. He was sure the magic charm wouldn't let him down.

At tea all the twins helped themselves in their usual fashion, which was to load their plates with as many as possible of their favourite things. Their mother always made them put them all back again, but it was worth a try.

Nick's approach was more subtle. He only ever had one sandwich or biscuit or bun or piece of cake actually on his plate, but always held two others in his left hand under the table.

He began on a big plate of sandwiches, peeling one back first to see what was inside. It was some pinkish stuff.

'What's in these, Mum?' he asked.

'Fish-paste.'

'They're nice.'

He took two more.

'What sort of fish?'

'I don't know exactly,' his mother said. 'The jar's in the kitchen. I'll fetch it when I go to fill the teapot.'

'"Delicious Fish-Spread",' she read out when she came back, holding the jar. '"Made with butter, spices, herbs, soya rusks, added vitamins, shrimp, tuna'(she turned the jar round to finish reading the label) 'oh, and a little salmon."''

The merrythought had granted Nick's wish.

'How clever of you,' he said to it later, holding it up. 'It was really an impossible sort of thing to ask for, yet you managed to get round it. Silly of me really, to be wishing for crazy things. I'm sure that's not the way I should be using you. I mean, if I said (and now Nick laid the wishbone flat on the palm of his hand, for safety's sake) '"I wish I could fly", then probably Dad would come and say we were all going on holiday to Spain in an aeroplane. But if I said "I wish I could fly" and then jumped out of the window, I'd only have myself to blame, not you.'

He put it away in its neat blue box. What a useful little box it is for keeping a bird's fused clavicles in, he thought as he put the lid on. Exactly the right size.

After school the following day it was once again raining. Nick was tempted to stop it, but then he remembered that, despite the downpour of a few days before, the farmers and gardeners were still short of water, and that his father had actually offered prayers for rain in church.

He didn't feel he should match a wish against a prayer, so he forgot about fishing or football on the lawn. Instead he watched some television and played a board game with the OTs and went to bed without actually opening the drawer in which the merrythought lived.

At breakfast next morning his mother said, 'Oh, I've suddenly remembered, Nick, I have a sin to confess.'

'Is it a very grave sin?' said the Vicar.

'Well, no. I'm sure Nick won't mind. It's just that I had to post Granny's present yesterday, Nick – it's her birthday tomorrow, remember? – and it was breakable, a lovely little fairing I found in the Antique Market in town, and I needed a strong little box to pack it in. Well, I knew you usually have lots to keep your modelling things in, and I found just the right one, in the drawer in your room. Exactly the right size.'

'Oh no, Mum!' said Nick. 'Not the blue one?'

'It was blue, yes.'

'But it had something in it.'

'Only an old bone.'

'It's not just an old bone . . . what did you do with it, Mum?'

'I threw it away. Does it matter? Nick, where are you going?' for with a cry of 'Oh no!' Nick had left his breakfast and dashed out of the room.

'It seems it was a very grave sin,' said the Vicar.

It's dustbin day, thought Nick as he rushed round to the back of the Vicarage, and the lorry always comes just before we go off to school. If only I'm in time! If only I can find it!

So feverishly was Nick scrabbling through the contents, searching madly among the hotchpotch of ashes and wrappers and tins and bottles and kitchen waste, that he did not hear the dustbin lorry rumble up. He was still head down in the bin when he felt a tap on his shoulder and looked up to see one of the dustmen standing there in his orange overalls.

'What're you lookin' for, son?' said the dustman.

'A bone!' gasped Nick.

'Hear that?' said the dustman to the driver. 'They

do say parsons is poorly paid. Here's this one's boy lookin' for bones in the bin – must be starvin' hungry, poor kid!' and with a loud laugh, he tipped the contents of the Vicarage dustbin into the back of the lorry.

When Nick came back into the room, he was a sight. His hands and arms were filthy, and down through the dust on his cheeks coursed twin runnels of tears.

The OTs' eyebrows shot up.

The NTs' mouths fell open.

Even the slimline Piglet gave a low whine of distress and crept away, his stub tail between his legs.

'Where *have* you been?' Nick's mother said.

'Looking for my bone,' sniffed Nick. 'In the dustbin.' He gulped. 'It's gone,' he said.

'Gone?'

'In the dustbin lorry. They've been.'

His mother smiled. 'Then you're in luck,' she said. 'I remember now, I put your precious old bone in the pedal-bin in the kitchen. I meant to empty it before breakfast, but I didn't. It'll still be there.'

'It's not like Nick to get so upset,' she said to her husband later, when the older children had set off to walk through the churchyard to the village school. 'And all over an old bone, a chicken's wishbone.'

'A part of one, d'you mean?' said the Vicar. 'They always pull them and break them.'

'No, he'd mended this one, glued the two bits back together. Odd that he should make such a fuss though. After all, it's not as if there could possibly be anything special about the thing.'

CHAPTER 5

'Could Do Better'

What a relief it had been to Nick to see the merry-thought safe among the rubbish in the pedal-bin! By the time he had cleaned himself up, it was too late to think of a new place to keep it, so he shoved it in his anorak pocket and took it to school with him.

Once there, of course, he started to worry about it, and kept wanting to check that it was all right. Three times in the first lesson he asked to go to the toilet, for the lavatories were next door to the cloak-room where the coats were hung; and at break, he wore his anorak in the playground, in spite of the fact that it was a very hot day.

After playtime he decided to put the merrythought in his trouser pocket, and then, of course, he began to worry that it would get broken. After all, it was a fragile thing. Deep in thought about this, he suddenly heard his teacher's voice.

'Nick!'

'Yes, sir?'

'What was I just saying?'

I wish I knew, thought Nick, but there was only one way of making that happen, so he sat and said nothing.

'Wake yourself up,' said the teacher, and to the rest of the class, 'we'll go through that again, for Nick's benefit.'

Once more he explained about triangles, and the names for ones with equal angles and ones with equal sides.

While he was doing so, Nick was feeling in his pocket to make sure the merrythought was unharmed. It seemed to be, but to be sure he smuggled it out, slowly and carefully, and behind the cover of his maths book, slid it on to the top of his desk. I should have left it at home, he thought, where it would be safe. But then it wasn't safe in the blue box, was it? Where shall I keep it now? I must find an absolutely safe hiding-place, where nobody . . .

'Nick!'

'Yes, sir?'

'What do we call a triangle that has equal sides?'

Instinctively, Nick took hold of the two ends of

the wishbone, but at that instant his teacher said, 'Whatever it is that you're playing with, give it here.'

Nick simply didn't have the courage to hold up the merrythought and say, 'I wish I didn't have to give it to you sir.' Instead, he walked up to the teacher's desk and handed it over.

The teacher held it up before the class.

'What is this?' he asked.

'A wishbone, sir,' someone said.

'A merrythought,' said somebody else.

'I don't suppose,' said the teacher, 'that you can tell us, Nick, what part of a chicken this object is? Can you?'

'Yes, sir. The fused clavicles.'

Nick's teacher looked at him for a long moment. Then he put the merrythought in a drawer and said, 'Come and see me here after lunch.'

At the end of lunch when the rest of the school was rushing around the playground, Nick came into the classroom. He'd hardly eaten anything (it had been chicken, to make things worse). Suppose the teacher was to confiscate his merrythought? He couldn't, could he? It's my property, after all, thought Nick, he's got to give it back to me. Hasn't he?

'Sit down, Nick,' said his teacher. 'It's time you and I had a little chat. You are not a stupid boy. In fact, you are a bright boy, and usually, you act quite sensibly. But over the last few weeks, you seem to have been in a dream. What's come over you?'

'Don't know, sir,' said Nick. (But I do, he thought. Over the last few weeks my mind has been on my magic merrythought.)

'You're not unhappy about anything, are you?'

'No, sir.' (Only that you've got my magic charm.)

'So what's the matter then?'

'Nothing.' (Nothing that I can tell you.)

The teacher sighed. He opened the drawer of his desk and took out the wishbone.

'I am not going to give this back to you,' he said

(and Nick opened his mouth to protest), 'yet,' (and Nick shut it again) 'or else you'll be playing with it all afternoon. Come and ask me for it when school ends and then you can have it back. All right?'

'Yes, sir. Thank you.'

The teacher held the wishbone by the tips of the arms of the V, between finger and thumb, as a dowser might hold his divining-rod when searching for water. He looked at it for a moment.

Then he said, 'You know Nick, I wish you would start to work really hard.' Then he almost dropped the merrythought.

'Odd,' he said, 'I could have sworn the thing moved. Must be imagining things.' He put the bone back in the drawer. 'Off you go,' he said. 'Run on out and play.'

'Sir,' said Nick, 'I'd rather stay in and work.'

'Heavens above!' said the Vicar when Nick brought home his school report at the end of term. 'Have you been converted?'

'What d'you mean, Dad?'

'You suddenly seem to have changed your *modus operandi*.'

'Sorry?'

'Your way of working. Listen to this.

Nick has a good brain which he does not always fully employ. He could do much better if he tried a little harder.

'Well, we've heard that one before.

Having said that, however, I am delighted to say that, over the latter part of the term, Nick has apparently decided to apply himself to his work, and has achieved excellent results in all subjects. His thoroughness, attention to detail and general enthusiasm has been marked, and his nose, in short, has been firmly applied to the grindstone. Well done!'

Nick stood silent, grinning somewhat sheepishly.

'Well done indeed!' said his father. 'I couldn't have wished for anything better.'

CHAPTER 6

Dangerous Hill

Since Nick had never actually said 'I wish I could fly' to the merrythought, the family did not go to Spain for their summer holidays for the first time, but went to Cornwall in the car as usual.

The Vicar's car was a very old, very long Volvo, into which everybody and everything was somehow packed. The Vicar drove, his wife sat beside him with Piglet on the floor at her feet. Behind them in the back Nick sat between the NTs, and behind them, in what was called 'the back-back', were the OTs, facing to the rear. Everyone except Piglet was strapped in, a mass of luggage was tied on the roof-rack, and the old car groaned its way to the South and West, heavily laden as a Middle Eastern donkey.

It was overtaken by practically every car on the road, occasionally receiving some strange looks from a number of other travellers, since the OTs liked making rude faces through the rear window.

Nick's job was to keep the NTs amused by playing games, like counting different coloured cars, or the pub game where you scored a point for every leg, human or animal, that appeared on a pub sign on your side of the road. He also had to deal with their constant questions, beginning, about a mile out from the Vicarage, with 'How much further?' and then – at regular intervals until at last, with luck, they dozed off in their straps – 'Are we nearly there?'

When they did fall asleep, Nick fell to reflecting upon the merrythought. Partly because of its extraordinary powers, partly because of the apparent energy he had felt in it each time it gave its wish-granting twitch, he had grown into the habit of thinking of it, not as the old bone of a dead bird, but as a living thing, a being, a personality with, in some mystical way, a mind of its own.

'I hope you won't be lonely,' he said to it at bedtime the previous evening. 'Being left on your own, I mean. It's only for two weeks, though, I'll soon be back. And, by the way, if you hear noises, don't worry – it'll only be young Mrs Pargeter's daughter Dolly. She's got the key so she can come in to water the houseplants.'

Then he put it back in its new home. This was a tiny wooden chest, a miniature coffer three inches long, two wide, and an inch and a half deep, which Nick had made and stained and varnished. More, he had ensured that it would be absolutely safe by using its future occupant to wish that no one would ever take it or indeed open it.

Even so, he had decided not to bring it to Cornwall. He had begun to feel that he was once more being tempted to use its magic purely selfishly, for his own ends, and that somehow this wasn't fair or right or sensible. Maybe it would always retain its powers and not lose them like the torch battery, but even so, Nick felt, it was best to keep them in reserve, for something really important, for the good of somebody else.

However, he had not been able to resist one last wish before they set out. You can't call this one selfish, he thought, because it's for all of us, and he said, 'I wish that we'll have lovely weather for our holiday in Cornwall.' He felt the merrythought give its little movement in reply, and then he laid it carefully in its coffer and closed the lid.

And now, as the Volvo rolled gallantly on, the sun shone down out of a cloudless sky, and Nick thought to himself with wonder – nobody knows except me that it's going to be like this for the whole two weeks, thanks to my marvellous merrythought.

47

And then at last, as they topped a hill, came the magic moment.

'Look!' cried the children's mother. 'I can see the sea!' and Piglet barked, and Josh and Cassandra stopped making faces and twisted round in their seats to look, and the NTs woke up.

'How much further?' said Denny, and 'Are we nearly there?' said Tim.

'Yes,' said Nick.

'Thank the Lord,' said the Vicar, and, patting the steering-wheel, 'Well done, good and faithful servant.'

How quickly the holiday flashed by! It seemed that they had hardly unloaded the car before they were loading it up again. And yet two whole weeks had gone by, two weeks of cream teas and Cornish pasties, of long days on the beach, building castles and fishing in the rock-pools and throwing sticks into the sea for the new, trim, active Piglet, and eating sandy Marmite sandwiches. And every day was lovely weather, just as Nick had wished, so that they were no sooner dry from one bathe than they wanted to rush into the water again. Nick was already a good swimmer, but by the end of the fortnight, both Cassandra and Josh had swum a number of strokes, and the NTs had made great strides with their armbands on.

Anyone seeing the family as they set off for home could have told they were coming back from holiday, for they were all as brown as berries. Only Piglet remained stubbornly white.

At about the half-way stage of the return journey, Nick was once more thinking of his merrythought and of how good it would be to take it out of its coffer – not necessarily to use it, but just to be happily re-united with it. He'd hardly thought of it at all in Cornwall – there was no need, he'd had everything he could wish for. And there's nothing I particularly need it for now, he was thinking, as they began the descent of a steep, twisting hill.

But how wrong he was.

At the top of the hill was a notice:

DANGEROUS HILL
SHARP BENDS
ENGAGE LOW GEAR
ESCAPE ROUTE $\frac{1}{2}$ MILE

and the Vicar put his foot on the brake.

Nothing happened.

Very quickly, for the gradient was very sharp, the heavy old Volvo began to pick up speed as the first bend loomed ahead.

'The brakes have gone!' said the Vicar to his wife, and the urgency in his voice set the NTs off crying, while in the back-back the OTs sat goggling at the sight of how quickly they were racing away from the next car behind them.

'Haul on the hand-brake!' cried the Vicar to his

wife, as with a crashing of gears he managed to change to a lower one, all of which only slowed them down a little as they whizzed round the first corner.

Nick stared in horror as they careered down the twisting hill. If only he had brought the merry-thought! If only he had it in his hands now, he could stop the car, somehow, he could save them from what promised to be the end of more than just a holiday. He watched his father wrestling the car round bend after bend, making desperate attempts to change into a still lower gear, which

only seemed to result in a further increase in speed.

Faster and faster they went and louder and louder was the wailing within as the OTs joined the NTs chorus of lament. Nick too was shouting in fear, and Piglet yapped madly.

At that moment another notice appeared on the left of the road.

**ESCAPE ROUTE
RUNAWAY VEHICLES ONLY**

Diverging from the road at a slight angle, fifty yards ahead, was a short stretch of track. In contrast to the grey of the tarmac, it was a yellowish colour, seemingly composed of coarse gravel. It ended in a steep bank, much as a railway siding ends in buffers, and to take it, it seemed, was merely to choose another way of crashing.

Everyone tensed themselves for disaster as the Vicar wrenched the speeding car off the road and on to the escape route.

'God help us,' he said between clenched teeth.

For a few seconds there was a great crunching and scrunching as the heavy Volvo ploughed into the deep yellow shingle. Then, settling deeper and deeper, it came to a grinding halt and lay like a beached whale.

The Vicar's wife turned to her husband. 'And He did,' she said.

CHAPTER 7

'Yours for 50p!'

None of the family ever forgot the end of that summer holiday – their terror in the runaway Volvo, their relief at their escape, all the long-drawn-out business of waiting for the AA and for a breakdown truck, and hiring a car to get them and their belongings home, where they arrived as exhausted as if they had never had a holiday in their lives.

Next day the Vicar set out on his old bicycle to visit his parishioners, and his wife took a bus to the shops.

'At least the children can walk to school when it starts next week,' she said. 'That's something, isn't it? But I'll be glad when we get the car back.'

'Heaven only knows what it's going to cost to mend it,' the Vicar said, and it wasn't long before he knew as well as heaven.

A couple of days later, he opened a letter at breakfast and said to his wife, 'Looks like the estimate for the repairs.'

He scanned it, and his wife, watching, saw his face fall.

'"Man is born unto trouble, as the sparks fly upward",' he said.

'Is it very bad?'

'Very bad. The entire braking system needs replacing, the suspension was damaged when we ploughed into that gravel, and as for passing the MOT (which is due shortly), they give a list of umpteen things that need doing. Moth and rust doth corrupt the poor old car. It's had it.'

'How much will it cost to mend it, Dad?' said Nick.

'Too much. It won't be worth mending. I'll just have to take whatever they offer me for it.'

'And buy a new car?' said Cassandra.

'A new Volvo?' said Josh.

'Can we have a red one?' said Denny.

'Can we get it tomorrow?' said Tim.

'With a bit of luck,' said the Vicar, 'they might give me enough to buy a new bicycle, and that's about the size of it.'

And he wasn't far wrong.

'Mum,' said Nick the following Sunday, while

54

they were doing the washing-up in Dad's Quiet Time, 'why can't we buy another car?'

His mother sighed.

'The old one only fetched a few hundred pounds,' she said, 'and Daddy's stipend is not exactly generous, you know. The trouble is, we need such a big car to take all of us, and big cars are expensive. We can only afford something pretty ancient, and I don't want any more brake failures, thank you. The sensible thing would be to buy a new one, but that's absolutely out of the question. It would cost the earth. Daddy could never pay for it.'

'Couldn't he pray for it?' Nick said.

His mother laughed.

'I don't think your father would approve of that suggestion,' she said. 'He'd probably say, "God helps them that help themselves". In other words, it's up to him to do something about the problem. Maybe he'll find some way to borrow enough money. Or he'll pay by instalments. Or something. But it may take a long time.'

'It needn't,' said Nick to the merrythought. 'It needn't take any time at all. You could fix it. Today. Or tomorrow at the latest, probably.'

He thought back over the seven wishes the merrythought had already granted. Leaving aside the lesser ones, the three main wishes, concerning old Mrs Pargeter, Piglet, and himself, were all working splendidly. He had really begun to enjoy his schoolwork and to take a pride in it, Piglet still only ate half as much as before, and as for old Mrs Pargeter, she had thrown away her sticks and was walking around the village, boasting about the telegram the Queen would send her in ten years' time.

The magic worked, no doubt about that.

But how on earth could he explain things to his father if a brand-new estate car suddenly appeared outside the front door of the Vicarage? He would have to confess to the merrythought's powers, and this he certainly did not want to do. Nor would Dad like it, he thought, from what Mum said. He would think it undeserved and unacceptable.

Nick held the merrythought in the proper manner, thinking carefully. Then he said, 'I wish you could find some way – a way that Dad couldn't mind – to get us a brand-new Volvo estate.'

The wishbone moved, as, Nick could hear, did the OTs, anxious for a game after Dad's Quiet Time. He put the magic charm back in its coffer and went down to play, confident that it would solve the problem for him.

Which it did, that very evening.

Nick was wanting to finish the construction of a model aeroplane, and needing something to protect the surface of his work-table, went to the cupboard in the kitchen where old newspapers were kept. He took the top one off the pile, but it was not till he spread it on his table that he saw what was written in large red print across the top of the front page of yesterday's *Daily Mail*. It said:

TO WIN A
NEW
ESTATE CAR
SEE
PAGE 6!

With a sudden thrill of excitement, Nick turned the pages, and read:

> The newest, the biggest, the most powerful,
> the most expensive Volvo estate car, the
> 760 Turbo, diesel-engined, with automatic
> transmission, price complete with all avail-
> able extras £26,995, can be yours for
> 50p!!! Read on!

Nick read on.

It was the usual sort of competition where a car's most important points are listed – such things as power steering, electric windows, central locking, air-conditioning, trip computers and anti-lock brakes – and you're required to put them into an order of priority. If you get them in the correct order, you win the car.

There were ten points, marked A to J.

Nick took the merrythought out. 'You've done it!' he said. 'You've found the way to get us a new car! Now all we've got to do is put these in the right order. But how? Or are you going to show me?'

He held the wishbone in the usual way and, lowering it to the surface of page 6, pointed its fused end at each letter in turn.

A, B, C, D, E and F produced no reaction from it, but at G it twitched, so Nick wrote the figure 1 against G. Then he repeated the operation, and this time the merrythought twitched at B. Nick wrote 2 against that, and continued until all the letters had been arranged 'in what must be,' he said, 'the correct order.'

He was about to fill in the space for name and address when it occurred to him that maybe they wouldn't let a nine-year-old have a car.

I'll have to get Mum to help, he thought. He put the merrythought away, cut the coupon out carefully, and went downstairs.

Choosing a time when his mother was alone in the kitchen, he showed her what he had done, and asked, could she put her name on the coupon?

'I've got the 50p,' he said.

His mother looked at the cutting, and smiled.

'You haven't a hope of winning a competition like this,' she said. 'The odds are a million to one against.'

'You never know,' Nick said. 'It would be nice if we did though, wouldn't it?'

'It certainly would! Wait a minute, you haven't completed this bit here.'

> In the event of a tie, the entrant who completes this sentence most satisfactorily (in not more than twelve additional words) will be adjudged the winner. 'THE VOLVO 760 TURBO ESTATE IS . . .'

Oh help, thought Nick, the merrythought may have given me the right order, but someone else might get it too and then think up a better ending to that sentence.

'I don't know what to put, Mum,' he said. 'You do it.'

'Well, let's see, doesn't much matter because you haven't got a chance ... how about – "THE VOLVO 760 TURBO ESTATE IS ... the car which has everything the modern motorist could possibly wish for"?'

She counted on her fingers.

'Exactly twelve extra words. OK?'

'Thanks, Mum. I'll post it straightaway,' said Nick.

His mother smiled as he went dashing off.

'That's 50p down the drain, old boy,' she said.

She never gave the matter another thought until a couple of weeks later, when the phone rang, and an unknown voice asked for her by name.

She came back into the kitchen, where the family was sitting having tea, and said, rather shakily, 'You'll never guess!'

'Old Mrs Pargeter's died,' said Cassandra.

'She got struck by lightning,' said Josh, 'and frizzled up like a burnt sausage.'

The NTs said nothing because their faces were crammed full of food, and Nick said nothing because his heart was in his mouth.

'It has to be a nice surprise,' said the Vicar. 'You look like the cat that's eaten the cream.'

'It's very nice,' said his wife, 'and very, very surprising. That was the *Daily Mail*.'

'The *Daily Mail*?' said the Vicar. 'I don't get it.'

'You will. How would you like a new estate car, value £26,995? I've just won one.'

CHAPTER 8
One Bad Wish

'Won one?' said the Vicar. 'What can you mean?'

His wife explained about the competition.

'And what's more,' she said, 'the *Daily Mail* has arranged with the nearest Volvo dealers to deliver it, here, tomorrow morning!'

At this all four twins grew very excited. Nick alone sat silent. Only now was he beginning to realize just what the merrythought had done this time. At odds of a million to one against, it had guided his hand to make the right selections in order to win a car costing almost twenty-seven thousand pounds! Beside this, all the other wishes it had granted were insignificant. He felt stunned. Which was what his father looked.

'It's a miracle,' said the Vicar dazedly to his wife. 'How in heaven's name did you manage to put all the various things in the correct order? You know as much about cars as I do, which is precious little.'

'I didn't do the selecting,' his wife said. 'Nick did all that. It's all thanks to him that we're getting it. They say that I won it because I put my name on the entry form, but really it's your car, Nick, isn't it?'

'Oh no,' Nick said. 'It's ours. It's for all of us. That's why I went in for the competition.'

'And spent his pocket-money on the entry fee too,' his mother said.

'Nick,' said his father, 'I simply don't know how we can thank you.'

Oh, don't thank me, thought Nick. It wasn't me that picked the right letters. For a second he was tempted to make a clean breast of the whole thing. But they wouldn't believe me anyway, he thought, so what's the point.

'It was just luck,' he said.

'Or Providence?' his father said. 'God moves in a mysterious way.'

And so, said Nick to himself, does the merry-thought.

But I suppose it's cheating really, he thought, lying in bed that night. I mean, just think of all the thousands of people who did the competition and would have loved to win, but they couldn't. They hadn't a hope because of the magic of my merry-thought. So it's not fair on them. But then maybe there were a whole lot of correct answers, so that they had to use the tie-breaker, and they thought Mum's sentence was the best? So really it was Mum who won it and not just the wishbone.

Reassured by this thought, he went to sleep.

By the next day, a Saturday, when the prize arrived, Nick was no longer worrying about the rights and wrongs of the matter. The car was here, and it was all theirs!

How gleamingly white was its shining paintwork, and how luxurious its black leather upholstery, and how richly and unmistakably new it smelt!

Then of course they all went for a ride in the beautiful monster, with its electrically operated win-dows and its power-assisted steering and its air-conditioning. And they switched on the radio, and would you believe it, a voice was singing 'Oh what a beautiful morning!'

'You have first go,' the Vicar had said to his wife. 'After all, you won it.'

'No, I didn't, Nick did and he can't drive. Anyway, I'd sooner you went first.'

In the end they took turns.

But the strangest thing of all about the new Volvo 760 Turbo Estate was its number-plate. Only Nick

noticed it, when they arrived home again, and he stood and gawped at it. His mother and the other children had gone into the Vicarage and his father was carefully wiping off a few insects that had had the cheek to die a messy death against the windscreen.

'Dad,' said Nick. 'Look.'

The Vicar came to inspect the number-plate. 'M 3110 NJW,' he read out. 'Well, I'm blowed!' he said. 'Your initials! Nicholas John Wilson.'

'And my birthday,' said Nick.

'How d'you mean? Oh, I see – 31.10 – the 31st of October. How absolutely extraordinary! A chance in a million.'

'Like winning the competition.'

'Yes. Amazing. The 'M', of course, is just this year's letter.'

Not just that, thought Nick. M stands for merrythought, and there's no limit to what it can do.

It occurred to him later, as he sat on the edge of his bed looking at the magic charm, that if it could make very good things happen, like the new car, it could also presumably make very bad things happen.

For the first time he felt suddenly frightened at the thought of the strange force within this bit of bone.

Suppose, instead of being his, it had belonged to someone wicked, like a terrorist, who might point it at a plane, an air-liner, say, packed with people. 'I wish that plane would crash,' the terrorist would say, and down it would fall, killing everyone on board. Or if a general used it, in a war, and wished all the enemy soldiers dead. Over they'd all go like ninepins. Because it worked when other people used it, if they held it right – his teacher had proved that. He must guard it with the greatest of care. He must always act sensibly about it.

'But it might be rather fun,' Nick said to the merrythought, 'to use you to make one bad wish, not a very bad one, just to see what happens.'

He looked out of his bedroom window to see the OTs playing with a football on the lawn. Their footballing consisted entirely of penalties. Cassandra took them all and Josh saved them if he could. The NTs stood well back behind Josh and retrieved the shots that he let through.

Nick stood looking down and thinking. He tried to think of a little bad wish, nothing that would hurt anyone of course, just something annoying, a bit mischievous. The children were playing at the far end of the lawn, where it began to slope down towards the stream at the bottom.

'I know!' said Nick suddenly. He held the merry-thought in the action position. 'I wish,' he said, 'that the football would go in the stream.'

And the merrythought jiggled, and Cassandra gave the ball a tremendous thump, and Josh missed it, and so did the NTs.

Tim, who was the nearest to it, turned and set off in pursuit.

Faster and faster he ran on his short fat legs as the ball went rolling on down the grassy slope and over the edge of the bank into the water. Unable to stop, Tim fell in with a splash.

Nick heard him give one loud gurgling cry, and then there was a horrid silence.

CHAPTER 9

A List of Presents

Nick went tearing downstairs, shouting 'Mum! Dad! Tim's fallen in the stream!' and raced across the lawn, his parents following. The idea of using the merrythought to ensure Tim's safety never occurred to him in his panic, though he still had it in one hand as he ran.

But in fact it was not needed.

By the time he arrived on the bank, both the OTs were already knee-deep in the water, each gripping one of their little brother's arms, while Denny hovered above, wide-eyed, crying, 'Timmy, Timmy, are you all right?'

He was, apart from having swallowed a lot of water. The silence that had succeeded his yell on tumbling in was because he had, for a moment, submerged, but the stream was a shallow one, and all that Tim had suffered was a thorough soaking and a bad fright.

'It was my fault,' said Cassandra, when they had hauled him out, coughing and spitting and snivelling. 'I kicked the ball too hard. I didn't know I could kick that hard.'

'It was my fault too,' said Josh. 'I should have saved it, but it was a screamer – I don't reckon Chris Woods could have stopped it.'

As for Denny, he just cried because Tim was crying.

'Cheer up, all of you,' their mother said. 'Come on, let's get everybody dried out.'

Nick went to retrieve the football, which had floated into an inlet a little further downstream.

'No harm done,' his father said when he came back, 'but that could have been nasty, you know. Suppose he'd hit his head on something when he fell in, or got tangled in some weeds. Children have drowned in a few inches of water before now.'

And it wouldn't have been the OTs fault but mine, thought Nick, looking at the merrythought which, he had just realized, he was still holding.

'Is that that old wishbone you glued together?' his father asked.

'Yes.'

'Do you make wishes on it?'

'Sometimes.'

'Just remember, Nick, it's only superstition, all that stuff. You can wish till you're blue in the face on a sprig of lucky heather or a four-leaf clover or a rabbit's foot or that old thing, but those sort of wishes don't come true, you know. And don't forget, there are bad wishes as well as good ones.'

'Yes, I know.'

'Listen, my old chap,' the Vicar said. 'If you really want something to happen, you have to have faith. St Matthew said that if you truly have faith, even the size of a grain of mustard seed, you can move mountains.'

He put his arm round Nick's shoulders as they turned to walk back up the lawn. 'And Matthew was talking about faith in God, not in some lucky charm like that old bit of bone,' he said. 'Can't think why you keep it.'

'It's just a mascot, Dad,' said Nick.

In the days and weeks that followed, Nick did a lot of thinking, about what his father had said, and about what the wishbone had done. And the more he thought, the more certain he became that whatever it said in the Bible, he had faith in the merry-thought. There was absolutely no doubt of its powers, for selfish ends or unselfish, for good or for bad. Talk about a grain of mustard seed, why, if he should ever hold the bone and stand at the foot of a mountain and wish that it would move, it would! Whatever happened – a landslide, an avalanche, a volcanic eruption, an earthquake – that mountain would jolly well move. The merrythought would do anything he asked of it, from curing old Mrs Pargeter to providing a brand-new estate car.

The thought of the car reminded him of its number-plate, and that in turn reminded him that his birthday was only a couple of weeks away.

What presents would he get? Why – unlike any other boy in the world – absolutely anything and everything he wanted!

From his mother and father, from his grandparents, from uncles and aunts, from anybody at all, he could, by the power at his command, simply order exactly what he fancied!

The most expensive model-making kits, a stereo system, a movie camera, a ten-speed bike, his own TV set – anything, no matter what it cost! He could have the lot.

After all, of the nine things for which the merrythought had so far been used – eight times by him, once by his teacher – only two wishes had been what you might call selfish. Scoring a goal was one and catching a salmon was the other, and a fat lot of use either of them had been. Surely now it was time, in celebration of his tenth birthday, to make the tenth wish a real bonanza! Nick was sorely tempted!

He sat down at his work-table and began to make out a list. There were two columns, one of costly presents and one of the people who, little did they know it, were going to give them. Only his sister and his brothers were let off lightly. Last year, he remembered, the OTs had given him a Mars bar each, and the NTs a packet of cheese-and-onion flavoured crisps between them, so he put them all down for a repeat. The last name on his list was that of a great-uncle who, at their only meeting, had given Nick a 5p piece as a parting present. Now he was down for a wristwatch that would set him back a thousand times that sum.

As Nick finished writing, the NTs came into his bedroom.

'What's that?' said Denny.

'A list.'

'What for?' said Tim.

'My birthday presents.'

'Let's see,' they said.

Nick handed it over, secure in the knowledge that they couldn't read, and they held it between them and scanned it in a critical manner.

'It's a long list,' said Tim.

'Yes.'

'A lot of presents,' said Denny.

'Yes.'

'You're lucky,' they said.

Aren't I just, thought Nick after they had gone – Wow! What a birthday this one is going to be!

Writing all the things down on paper had somehow made each seem that much more desirable. He would jolly well have the lot!

All thoughts of acting sensibly had vanished. Nick was drunk with the power of the merrythought.

He closed the door, opened the drawer, and took it out of its little wooden coffer. Then he sat down at his work-table, the list of presents in front of him, the ends of the wishbone held lightly between fingers and thumbs.

'I wish,' he said, 'that on my birthday . . . ' but before he could utter another word, the merry-thought jumped, literally jumped, it seemed, out of his grasp and fell on to the table.

Nick had grown used to its customary little twitch on granting a wish, but this was totally different, more sudden, stronger. There was no question of Nick persuading himself that he had dropped it. It had definitely reacted sharply to something that he had said.

It can only have been the word 'birthday', Nick thought. I'll try putting it differently.

He picked the merrythought up again, held it correctly once more, and said, 'I wish that on October the 31st . . .' and instantly it leapt out of his hands again on to the table, but this time it landed slap in the middle of the list of presents and lay there. Nick could almost have sworn it gave a little shiver.

For the third time he picked the bone up, a little gingerly now, so convinced was he of the life-force within it. He held it up by its fused part and said to it, 'You're angry with me, aren't you?'

Slowly the two ends of the wishbone turned down, just like a dowser's divining-rod turns down to point to water. They were pointing at the list.

There was no mistaking what the merrythought meant.

Nick sighed.

'All right,' he said. 'I get you. I'm being too selfish, aren't I? You just think I'm too greedy, isn't that it?'

Slowly the two ends returned to the horizontal.

Nick put the merrythought down on the table, picked up the list of presents, tore it into small pieces, and dropped them into the waste-paper basket. He sat for a while, thinking.

He was in no doubt of the merrythought's disapproval – it had shown it all too plainly. But how had it managed to do all that jumping about and pointing? Where did it get the energy?

From me, it must be from me, he thought, just as

the divining-rod gets its energy from the dowser. So that must mean that I disapprove too, that I know in my heart of hearts that to go asking for a whole lot of expensive things for myself is wrong and greedy and something to be ashamed of. Which, come to think of it, I suppose I am.

He picked the merrythought up again.

'Right,' he said to it. 'Let's forget all about birthday presents. We'll wish for something simple and easy, shall we? How about something for my sister and my brothers? A nice treat of some sort. Well, that's got to be food, of course. Mum's out shopping at the moment – we'll make her buy a nice surprise for tea, something that both the OTs and the NTs particularly like. And what's more, it had better be something I'm not very fond of, and then you can't accuse me of being selfish. Let's think. I know! Swiss roll – a big chocolate one with that creamy stuff inside. I don't much like them, I like the plain sponge ones with jam. I could ask for a little one of those, I suppose. No, better not.'

He picked up the wishbone and said, 'I wish that there'll be a big chocolate Swiss roll for tea.' He held the ends of the bone rather more tightly than usual in case it should misunderstand him, but it only gave its customary slight movement to show that the matter was under control.

'Ooo look!' cried the NTs and 'Yummee!' said the OTs at the tea table, as their mother came in with a big chocolate Swiss roll on a plate.

'I suddenly thought,' she said to Nick, 'that this is the twins' favourite. I know you don't much like it.'

'That's OK, Mum,' said Nick.

His mother smiled.

'It is, actually,' she said, and she went back to the kitchen and returned with another plate.

On it was another Swiss roll, a small sponge one with jam.

CHAPTER 10
Start the Clock

'It's only a couple of weeks till your birthday, Nick,' his mother said at breakfast next morning. 'What d'you want from Dad and me? Another construction kit or what?'

'I don't know,' Nick said.

'That's not like you,' his father remarked. 'Usually you are very precise about what you want.'

'I'd rather it was a surprise,' Nick said.

'*We're* going to give you a surprise,' said the OTs and the NTs with one voice.

'I bet.'

'We'll have to see what we can do,' the Vicar

said. He ate the last bit of his toast and marmalade, drank the rest of his coffee, and looked at his watch. It said 8.45. Then, automatically, he looked out of the window at the clock on the south face of the church tower. It said four o'clock. It had said four o'clock for six weeks.

'Do you realize,' his wife said, 'that almost without fail you still check the time on your watch with the church clock? It's as though you were expecting it to have started going again, by magic.'

'I wish it would,' the Vicar said.

Granted, thought Nick.

'What's the matter with it, Dad?' he said. 'Can't you wind it up?'

'It's fully wound, actually,' his father said, 'but some part of the mechanism is jammed. Or that's what the horological engineer says.'

'The who?'

'Just a posh name for a clock-mender. This one's a specialist in tower clocks, and he says he won't fiddle about with ours in its present state. According to him, it all needs stripping down and cleaning and re-assembling, and his estimate for the work is £1,500. There just isn't that sort of money available. I really must do something about launching an Appeal to see if we can raise enough.'

No need, said Nick to himself. I'll be back from school in plenty of time to fix it for you.

Just before four o'clock that afternoon, anyone crossing the lawn and looking towards the Vicarage

would have seen two figures standing and looking out. Downstairs, the Vicar was gazing from his study window at the church and trying to frame in his mind the wording of an Appeal for money to set matters right.

Upstairs, immediately above, Nick stood in his bedroom, wishbone at the ready, his eyes on his digital watch. It read 3.59.

'£1,500!' sighed the Vicar. 'How shall we ever collect that much?' He raised his eyes. 'We need help from above,' he said.

'I wish,' said Nick as the figures on his watch turned to 4.00, 'that our church clock would start again.'

Even as the merrythought twitched, the first chime of the hour rang out from the tower.

Nick put the wishbone away in its coffer and ran downstairs, to find his father standing on the lawn, staring in amazement at the church tower.

'Did you hear that, Nick?' he said. 'The clock's started again. It just struck four,' and as they watched, they saw the long hand move to one minute past the hour.

'Heaven only knows how that happened,' said the Vicar.

'Funny,' said Nick. 'Only just now I was wishing it would,' but his father, he could see, was not listening.

Shall I tell him, Nick thought? I did it. I started the old clock up. I saved him having to find £1,500.

Not to mention winning him a £27,000 car. It was all my doing. There's nothing I can't do.

'Dad,' he said.

'What?'

'I did it.'

'Did what?'

'Made the clock go.'

'Oh, don't talk such rubbish, Nick.'

'I did! I did it with my magic merrythought. That's what saved old Mrs Pargeter's life and stopped Piglet being piggy and started me working harder and loads of things, including winning the new Volvo.'

'Oh, Nick,' said his father in a bored tone of voice. 'Do try and act sensibly.'

'I *knew* you wouldn't believe me,' said Nick. 'Wait here a minute, Dad. I'll show you.'

He ran upstairs and came back with the merry-thought.

'Now,' he said to his father, 'hold it like this . . . see . . . and then say out loud, "I wish . . ." whatever you like.'

'I'd like a cup of tea, that's what I'd like.'

'Go on then.'

'Oh, if I must,' said the Vicar, and he took hold of the bone.

'I wish it was teatime,' he said.

'Teatime!' called his wife from the house.

'Amazing,' said the Vicar drily.

'Odd though,' he said. 'The thing seemed to move.' He gave it back.

'It does,' said Nick. 'That was too easy, Dad. Wish for something else.'

'I wish I knew what to get you for your birthday,' his father said. 'It makes it so difficult when you won't say what you want.'

'That's OK, the merrythought will tell you,' said Nick. 'Here, have another go.'

The Vicar shook his head ruefully.

'What a lot of mumbo-jumbo,' he murmured, but all the same he took hold of the wishbone and said in a very sceptical voice, 'I wish that this piece of old bone will give me the inspiration needed to select the right birthday present for my eldest son, Nicholas John Wilson.'

'Great!' said Nick as the merrythought twitched. 'That's fixed that.'

CHAPTER 11

Birthday Surprise

'A camera,' said Nick to the merrythought.

He had just put it back in its coffer and was about to close the lid when it occurred to him that he ought to tell it his idea of the right birthday present. But then he realized that inspiration would have come to his father at the moment of wishing.

'A camera,' said the Vicar to his wife.

'What about it?'

'For Nick's birthday present. He said he'd like a surprise. It suddenly came into my head, just now, when I was standing on the lawn.'

'What a good idea,' his wife said. 'And what's more, I think we should splash out a bit and get him a really good one.'

'They can be horribly expensive,' said the Vicar doubtfully.

'So can Volvo 760 Turbo estate cars. It was Nick who got you that.'

'You're right,' said the Vicar. 'We owe him a great deal. I did have terrible misgivings at the time, you know – about accepting something so valuable. Very few people can afford such a thing.'

'Very few people,' said his wife, 'can afford to keep a wife, five hungry children, and a great rambling Vicarage on a stipend like yours. That car was heaven-sent, and I should have been furious if you had turned it down. You may leave the buying of the camera to me.'

'Yes, dear,' said the Vicar.

'Incidentally,' said his wife, 'I thought I heard the church clock strike just now. Was I imagining things?'

'No, dear,' said the Vicar. 'It started going again. I wish I knew why.'

In the two weeks before his birthday, Nick used the merrythought a lot. He didn't quite know why. It was almost as though the magic charm was somehow willing him to take it out of its coffer, and hold it, and wish, as if it was saying to him, 'Make hay while the sun shines.'

He used it for quite small, simple tasks, making the sun shine, for instance on the day of a wedding that his father was conducting, bringing rain (at night) because his mother said she needed it for the garden, ensuring that the OTs found their precious football which had been lost in the shrubbery, and so brainwashing the NTs before a visit to the dentist that they came back saying they'd had a lovely time and when could they go again?

He used it such a lot, in fact, that one morning, the day before his birthday, he became careless and forgot to put it back into the coffer and then into the drawer. Hearing his mother calling him, he ran downstairs, leaving the merrythought on his work-table.

'D'you think you could go down to Pargeter's for me, Nick?' his mother said. 'I've forgotten some things for a cake I'm going to make. A rather special cake.'

'For my birthday,' said Nick with a smile.

'Yes. Here's a list. And mind how you cross the street, some of those big lorries go right up on the pavement. I don't know where the other children are, but if you see them and they want to go with you, tell them "No".'

As it happened, Josh and the NTs were playing hide-and-seek in the churchyard. It was an ideal place for this game. There were hundreds of head-stones to crouch behind, and besides these, you could climb on to the top of one of several big stone coffins and lie flat, hoping the seekers would not look up. There were all sorts of other hiding-places too, like bushes and big dark yew trees and little doorways set in the sides of the church. One day the sexton, after drinking a cup of coffee from his thermos flask in the vestry, had come back, spade in hand, to complete the digging of a new grave, and had got the shock of his life to see a body (Josh) lying stock-still at the bottom of it.

Now Nick, seeing the three boys playing there, took a roundabout way to the village. There was no sign of Cassandra, and it did not occur to him to wonder where she was. It was just as well he could not know that at that very moment she was sitting at his work-table, holding the merrythought.

The day had started badly for Cassandra.

First, she had torn her jeans.

Second, she had been told off for tearing her jeans.

Third, she had been told to mend them herself.

'I can't!' she said. 'I don't know how!'

'Yes, you do,' her mother said. 'You've seen me mending things often enough and it's high time you had a go yourself, a great girl like you, nearly seven. You'll find some patches in my sewing-box.'

So Cassandra had stumped upstairs in a sulk, made worse by hearing the others going off to play.

It's not fair, she said to herself. Just because I'm a girl. If it had been one of the others, Mum would have done it for them. I wish I wasn't the only girl. I wish I had some sisters.

On her unwilling way to fetch the sewing-box, she passed Nick's open door and went in, thinking perhaps to get some sympathy from him. But he was not there. Then she noticed the wishbone. She sat down at Nick's work-table, and picked the bone up by its two ends, not really thinking what she was doing, her mind still full of the unfairness of being the only girl among a pack of boys.

'Mending my own clothes!' she said bitterly. 'Next thing, she'll be making me do the washing and the ironing. And the cooking. And the housework. Boys are lucky, boys are.'

She stared moodily out of the window, still holding the merrythought. 'I wish I had some sisters,' she

said in a very grumpy voice. Then she jumped as the merrythought twitched, twice.

When Nick came back from running his errand, there was nothing to show that anyone had been in his room.

'Silly me,' he said, 'to leave the merrythought out like that. One of the others could have got hold of it.'

He was about to put it in its coffer, but then he changed his mind and gave way to temptation. If I make it vague enough, he thought, surely I could wish for *something* for myself, for my birthday?

'Now don't go jumping about all over the place,' he said to the wishbone. 'And don't worry – I haven't made another list of presents. All I'm going to ask for is something unexpected, just for fun,' and he held it correctly and said, 'I wish for a really smashing surprise tomorrow.'

The merrythought twitched a long shuddering twitch.

At breakfast Nick opened his birthday presents, beginning with family ones from grandparents and uncles and aunts.

Then he opened what were clearly the twins' ideas of surprises, for the OTs had given him not Mars, but Crunchie bars, and the NTs packet of crisps was scampi-flavoured.

Last of all, he undid the parcel labelled 'Happy birthday and much love from Mum and Dad'. If only you knew, thought Nick as he unknotted the string, I know exactly what's in here.

But when the paper came off, he gave a gasp of amazement. It was not the modest little beginner's model he'd expected. It was a Pentax Zoom 60! The merrythought had done its stuff.

'What a really smashing surprise!' he cried.

The very first picture he took, before setting off for school, was of his marvellous magic charm in its wooden coffer. As he did so, he noticed that a minute screw was missing from one of the pairs of tiny brass hinges that closed the coffer's lid. He searched everywhere for it, but to no avail.

'I'll mend you after school,' he said. 'I know Dad's got some screws that size in his workshop.'

There were a lot of outbuildings attached to the Vicarage, including an old coach-house. This was nowadays used as a garage, and because it was so wide, the Vicar had fixed up one side of it as a workshop, with a long workbench, above which were rows of cupboards.

Back from school, Nick fetched the coffer and its contents, put it down on the bench, and began opening some of the old tobacco-tins in which his father kept all different sizes of nails and screws. While he was searching for a really tiny screw, Piglet came into the coach-house and began sniffing about under the bench. Here were stored all kinds of odds and ends in an army of cardboard boxes, and soon

Piglet began to show particular interest in one of them. He snuffled loudly at it, and then started to scratch at it and whine.

By now Nick had found a screw that looked small enough.

He took the wishbone out of the coffer and laid it on the edge of the bench. He was just about to fit the screw when he heard, above the loud yapping that the dog was now making, the sound of the Volvo as his father returned from a visit.

Then everything happened at once.

The cause of Piglet's excitement, a mouse, made a bolt for it.

Piglet, rushing out from under the bench in hot pursuit, dashed straight between Nick's legs.

Nick, caught off balance, dropped the screw, and whipped round suddenly to see where it had fallen and to shout angrily at the dog. As he did so, his sleeve brushed the merrythought and sent it spinning off the bench and out on to the concrete floor, right in the path of the approaching car.

The Vicar, driving in to the coach-house to see his eldest son make a wild and seemingly suicidal leap right in front of him, stood on the brakes. The heavy white car stopped dead in its tracks. But not in time.

The merrythought lay directly in the path of the nearside front wheel, and before Nick could snatch it up, the tyre rolled over it.

There was a sudden sharp scrunching noise.

'Nick!' cried his father, leaping out of the car. 'Are you all right? What were you doing, jumping in front of the car like that? I didn't hurt you, did I?'

'No, Dad,' said Nick. 'You didn't hurt me.'

He knelt by the side of the little heap of tiny splinters which was all that was left of his magic merrythought.

This, then, was the really smashing surprise.

CHAPTER 12

Bon Voyage

'It's smashed,' said Nick in a choked voice.

The Vicar dropped to his knees beside his son and put an arm round Nick's shaking shoulders.

At that moment Denny's face appeared round the coach-house door. For a couple of seconds he stared round-eyed at the scene before him, and then was gone. The Vicar looked down at the splinters of bone.

'Your merrythought,' he said.

'Yes.'

'Oh, Nick, my dear boy. I'm so sorry.'

'It wasn't your fault,' said Nick.

He brushed the back of his hand across his eyes, and they both stood up. Nick turned to the work-bench and picked up the coffer.

'I was just fitting a screw,' he said, suiting the action to the words, 'when Piglet sort of tripped me up and I knocked the merrythought on to the floor. So it was all my fault.'

He closed the lid of the empty little box.

'Did you make that?' asked his father.

'Yes.'

'It's beautiful. What a clever old chap you are.'

It's a miniature coffer, he thought, a chest for holding treasure. But the treasure is no more.

He stood watching as Nick knelt down once again and began to pick up the tiny fragments of bone one by one and put them into the little wooden box.

Denny meanwhile had found his twin brother.

'Timmy,' he said, 'Nick can't come and play.'

'Why not?' said Tim.

'He's saying his prayers.'

'Saying his prayers at teatime?'

'Yes. And Daddy too. In the garage. They were kneeling down by the car.'

Cassandra and Josh appeared.

'Don't go in the garage,' Tim said.

'Why not?' said the OTs.

'Daddy and Nick are saying their prayers. Denny just saw them.'

'At teatime?' said Josh. 'Whatever for?'

'Don't you know?' said Cassandra.

'No,' they all said. 'Why?'

'You're thick, you are,' said Cassandra scornfully to her brothers. 'They were praying for something nice for tea.'

What the Vicar was in fact praying for at that moment was that Nick would not take this little tragedy too much to heart. He knew, as the others in the family did not, of Nick's belief in the magic powers of the merrythought, and he realized what a blow its loss must be.

He could not share that belief – his own faith and plain common sense told him that any success the boy imagined he had had through wishing on an old piece of bone was nothing more than coincidence. And yet . . . might there not be more things in heaven and earth than were dreamt of in his philosophy?

'You really did believe in it, didn't you?' he said, as Nick picked up the last minute fragment and dropped it into the coffer and closed the lid.

Nick nodded.

'You're not going to try and mend it, surely?'

Nick shook his head.

'It's like Humpty Dumpty, I'm afraid,' his father said. 'All the king's horses and all the king's men couldn't put that lot together again. You'll have to find some other use for that little coffer.'

'I'm going to,' Nick said. 'I'm going to use it for a coffin.'

'Bury it, you mean?'

'Yes.'

Not in the churchyard, I hope, thought the Vicar.

'Where?' he said, and he must have sounded anxious for Nick said, 'Don't worry. Not in the churchyard. Somewhere in the garden. Will you help, Dad?'

'Of course,' said his father. 'Funerals are all part of my job.'

'I don't want the others to know,' Nick said. 'Not even Mum. It's just a secret between you and me, Dad.'

'Right.'

'Promise?'

'Yes. But I want you to promise me something in return.'

'What?'

'Not to get too downhearted about what's happened. You're unhappy now, of course, and it's right and proper that people should mourn when they suffer loss, but I want you to act sensibly about this. What's done is done, and you're going to have to get used to life without magic.'

'I know,' Nick said. 'That's why I want to bury this.'

'Out of sight, out of mind, eh?'

'Yes.'

The thought of cremation as an alternative to interment crossed the Vicar's mind.

'We could burn it if you like,' he said. 'It's Guy Fawkes Day next week – I've already started preparing the bonfire. We could slip it in there. It just seems a bit of a shame, though, to destroy such a nice piece of workmanship.' He took the coffer from Nick and turned it in his hands. What other way was there to dispose of the dear departed? Burial at sea? And then a line from the Book of Ecclesiastes came into his head: 'All the rivers run into the sea.'

'Nick,' he said, 'I've just had a brainwave. What d'you think of this for an idea?'

So it was that after tea Nick and his father made their way down the Vicarage lawn to the stream. They had sneaked out quietly without attracting the notice of the rest of the family. They were wearing gumboots. Nick carried the little wooden coffer, and round his neck was slung the new Pentax Zoom 60.

They came to the bottom of the lawn and waded out into the middle of the stream. It was running strongly, for there had been quite a bit of rain recently (always at night, strangely enough).

Nick handed the coffer to his father.

'Could you hold it open, please, Dad?' he said. 'I took a photo this morning before I went to school, when the merrythought was . . . was all in one piece. But I just somehow feel I'd like to take one more.'

'Of course,' the Vicar said.

He opened the lid and tilted the coffer a little towards the camera, very cautiously in case any of

99

the dozens of splinters that he could see within should fall from their last resting-place.

Nick pressed the button. 'Right, you can shut it up now,' he said, and he took the coffer back and wound a thick elastic band round and round it to keep it shut. 'Shall I let it go now, Dad?' he said.

'Come a little nearer to me,' the Vicar said. 'The current's faster just here. Give me your other hand.'

Should I say something, he thought? 'We commit this bone to the deep'? No, that would be blasphemy. Better say nothing.

Should I say something, Nick thought? Can't think of anything except 'Goodbye and thanks'. No, that would be silly. Better say nothing.

He laid the coffer carefully upon the surface of the water, and let it go. Hand in hand, father and son stood watching in the evening sunshine, as the strange little craft sailed steadily away down the sparkling stream, spinning gently in the current as it went, and growing gradually tinier, until at last it vanished from their sight.

Nick spent the last hour of that tenth birthday taking photographs with his new camera, while there was still light.

He took them of his mother, of his father, of the OTs together, and the NTs together, and of Cassandra and Josh and Denny and Tim separately, and of Piglet, and of the Volvo, and that was the end of the film.

Next day it was taken to the photographer's shop in town to be developed, and a couple of days after that, the prints came back.

Nick took them up to his room.

Most of the snapshots were not at all bad, considering that he was a beginner. The joint one of the OTs was rather spoiled because they were both making silly faces, and in the individual ones of the NTs, Denny was without any feet, and Tim had no head.

At the bottom of the pile of a dozen prints were the two he had taken of the wishbone. Nick looked at the very first picture he had taken.

There, in the open coffer standing on the chest-of-drawers in his bedroom, brilliantly clear in the light of the built-in flash, was the familiar pale polished V of the merrythought, still all in one piece.

'The last sight of you,' he said, and reached for the final photo, taken in midstream as his father held up the coffer-turned-coffin with its sad content of little splinters.

I don't really want to look at this, Nick thought. I don't know what made me take it. But he made himself look, and he never forgot the shock it gave him. There was his father (or rather the middle of his father, for it was a close-up) standing in the stream, holding the open coffer.

But in it there were no little splinters.

In it was the familiar pale polished V of the merrythought. The shape of it was shadowy, transparent almost, but cameras can't lie, can they?

The merrythought was all in one piece once more.

When the photographs were shown to the family, the Vicar alone noticed that they only numbered ten. Afterwards, when they were by themselves, he said to Nick, 'What about the two you took of the wishbone in its coffer? Didn't they come out?'

'The one I took in my bedroom did.'

'What about the one in the stream, when I was holding it?'

'Something went wrong with that one,' Nick said.

'Can I see it?' asked his father.

Nick hesitated.

Then he went and fetched the photo, and handed it over.

The Vicar looked at it.
Then he looked at his son.
'Looks all right to me,' he said.

CHAPTER 13

The More, the Merrier

'George,' said the Vicar's wife to her husband on Christmas Eve.

'Yes, Annabel?'

'I think we should tell the children.'

'I'm surprised they haven't noticed,' said the Vicar. 'You're already quite a size, if you don't mind me saying so. I should have thought that Nick at any rate would have twigged you're having an-other baby.'

'George,' said his wife.

'Yes, Annabel?'

'I think I should tell you something.'

'What? Nothing wrong, is there? When you went to the hospital yesterday, I mean – everything was OK wasn't it? The baby's all right, isn't it?'

'The babies are all right,' said his wife.

The Vicar gulped. 'The more, the merrier,' he said bravely.

The boys obviously shared this view.

'Twins!' cried the NTs excitedly.

'Twin boys!' shouted Josh hopefully.

'Well done, Mum,' said Nick. 'At this rate, we'll have a football team before long.'

Only Cassandra said nothing.

'They could both be girls though, Mum, couldn't they?' she said to her mother later.

'I'll tell you something, Cass,' her mother said, giving her a cuddle. 'Between you and me and the gatepost, I've got a very strong feeling that they are.'

Quite suddenly Cassandra remembered the wish she had made, in Nick's bedroom, the day before his birthday, almost exactly eight weeks ago.

That old wishbone of his that she'd been playing with! It had jumped twice! It had to be a magic one! Just think, if Nick had only known that it had magic powers!

She ran off to find him.

'Nick?' she said.

'Yes, Cass?'

'You've got a wishbone, haven't you – a whole one I mean?'

'No, Cass. I did have one, but it got busted.'

'Oh,' said Cassandra.

What a shame, she thought. He can never have known it was a magic one. 'I ought to have told you,' she said. 'I saw it once. In your room. And I made a wish on it.'

'Did you?' said Nick. 'What was it?'

'I wished I could have some sisters. Nick, d'you think . . . ?'

'I don't think, Cass,' said Nick. 'I know. The new babies, I can tell you now, are absolutely positively definitely certain to be girls. The GTs.'

CHAPTER 14
Happy Christmas

'For what we are about to receive,' said the Vicar, 'may the Lord make us truly thankful.'

He picked up the carving knife and began to sharpen it upon the steel.

'I think I feel hungrier at Christmas lunch,' he said, 'than on any other day in the year.'

'No wonder,' his wife said. 'You have an awful lot to do on Christmas Day.'

The Vicar set to work, carving the turkey.

It was a large bird, and not surprisingly, its wishbone was a big one.

'Now then,' said the Vicar, 'whose turn is it for the merrythought?'

'Ours!' said the OTs and the NTs with one voice, but Nick said, 'No, it's not, Dad, it's mine. The NTs got it last time we had chicken.'

'Yes, they did,' his mother said.

'Who are you going to pull it with then, Nick – Mum or me? Or do you want to keep it all in one piece?' said his father, smiling.

Nick grinned at him.

'No, I don't want my turn, Dad,' he said. 'You pull it with Mum.'

'What's up, Nick?' his mother said. 'Don't tell me you're too old and grown up to believe in magic?'

'Oh no, Mum,' said Nick. 'I shan't ever be.'